Stratford Library Association
2203 Main Street
Stratford, CT 06615
203-385-4160
P9-DBO-792

SORCERER OF THE WAVES

SORCERER OF THE WAVES

by Kim Wilkins

illustrated by D. M. Cornish

Random House New York

This is a work of fiction. Names, characters, places, and incidents either are the product of the author's imagination or are used fictitiously. Any resemblance to actual persons, living or dead, events, or locales is entirely coincidental.

Text copyright © 2006 by Kim Wilkins
Illustrations copyright © 2006 by D. M. Cornish

All rights reserved.
Published in the United States by Random House Children's Books, a division of Random House, Inc., New York. Originally published in Australia by Omnibus Books, an imprint of Scholastic Australia Pty. Ltd., Gosford, in 2006.

Random House and colophon are registered trademarks of Random House, Inc.

Visit us on the Web!
www.randomhouse.com/kids

Educators and librarians, for a variety of teaching tools, visit us at
www.randomhouse.com/teachers

Library of Congress Cataloging-in-Publication Data
Wilkins, Kim.
Sorcerer of the waves / by Kim Wilkins ;
illustrated by D. M. Cornish. — 1st ed.
p. cm. — (The sunken kingdom ; bk. 3)
Summary: When Asa and Rollo discover that Ragni, a sorcerer who has been chained to a rock by the evil Emperor Flood, may know the fate of their parents, they set off in their invisible boat to find him.
ISBN 978-0-375-84808-7 (pbk.)
ISBN 978-0-375-94808-4 (lib. bdg.)
[1. Brothers and sisters—Fiction. 2. Magic—Fiction. 3. Fantasy.]
I. Cornish, D. M. (David M.), ill. II. Title.
PZ7.W64867So 2008
[Fic]—dc22 2007037000

PRINTED IN MALAYSIA
10 9 8 7 6 5 4 3 2 1
First Edition

Random House Children's Books supports the First Amendment and celebrates the right to read.

For Luka

CONTENTS

CHAPTER 1

A NIGHT JOURNEY

Whump!

Rollo fell to the ground, his sword flying out of his hands. A moment later, the tip of his opponent's blade hovered an inch in front of his nose.

"What did I tell you, Rollo?" demanded a gruff voice.

"Defend first," Rollo gasped. "Attack second."

The blade was pulled away and Skalti Wolfkiller's

warm hand yanked Rollo to his feet. "That's right," the big tide stealer said with a grin. "I know you're eager to get a strike in, but you must always think first of blocking blows. It hurts to get hit with a sword, Rollo. It hurts a lot. Don't forget that."

Rollo was embarrassed. Although he had been learning sword-fighting for two weeks, he always forgot this most basic of rules: defend yourself first; see what your opponent is capable of before you lash out with your own weapon. He dusted himself off. It was late afternoon and a stiff breeze from the sea danced in the branches that hid the entrance to Two Hills Keep.

"Now let's try again," Skalti said, tossing his sword from hand to hand. "Watch your six defense zones."

Rollo lifted his sword and the steel caught the glow of the sunset. Skalti had stolen this sword from the lair of the sea giants. The blade was short, the hilt carved from black stone.

"Ready?" he asked.

Rollo nodded and Skalti began to strike. Rollo

fended off blows to his head, the back and front of his neck, and all the other zones down to his thighs.

"Good. Now . . ." Skalti lifted his sword and lunged forward again. This time, Rollo blocked. Once, twice, three times. With the last block, he managed to force Skalti's sword up and out of his hands. It clanged to the ground four feet away.

Skalti laughed. "Well done," he said, rubbing his sore shoulder. "Very well done."

"Rollo!" It was his aunt Katla's voice, calling from the front door. "Come on, you two. It's getting cold."

She was right. Rollo shivered. Night was coming; the air was salty and moist. He sheathed his sword and headed inside. Skalti followed him.

"I've made a rabbit stew for dinner," Katla said to Skalti.

"I can't impose on you for too much longer," he said gently.

"Nonsense. You'll stay until you are well."

Rollo smiled to himself. Since the day he and his sister Asa had brought Skalti home with them, his shoulder injured in a fight with sea giants, Katla had grown very fond of the tide stealer. Even finding out that he was an undersea pirate hadn't changed her opinion of him. And, Rollo suspected, Skalti was growing fond of Katla, too.

Asa wouldn't hear of it, though. That night, after Katla had come to tuck them in and blow out their lantern, Rollo snuck out of bed.

"Asa?" he said, sitting next to her pillow. "Are you awake?"

"I am now," she grumped, and sat up.

"I need to ask you something."

"Well, try to be quiet. We don't want to wake Una." She nodded at the little bed where their baby sister slept. Rollo strained his eyes in the dark. Una's thumb was firmly jammed in her mouth and her eyelashes formed two dark curves on her plump cheeks.

"It's about Skalti and Katla," Rollo whispered.

"Not this again," Asa groaned. She flipped back her blankets so Rollo could climb into bed next to her.

"I think they're in love," he said.

"You're imagining it," she said, putting her arm around him and yawning.

"She gets this gooey look on her face whenever he's nearby," Rollo pointed out.

"Aunt Katla's just a very kind woman."

"And Skalti's a good man."

"Yes . . . ," Asa said slowly. "He's been good to us, but he is a tide stealer. A thief and a cutthroat. I don't believe that Aunt Katla would fall in love with anyone like that."

Rollo sighed. "Asa, you don't believe in *anything*."

"At least I'm not gullible like you."

"What does *gullible* mean?"

"It means you believe things without any proof."

"I *do* have proof," he protested. He threw back the covers and dragged her out of bed. "Come on, I'll show you."

"Where are we going?" she asked.

"To spy on them." He opened the door a crack. From up here they could see across the little landing and down into the corner of the kitchen. He could hear Skalti and Katla talking, but could not see them. The fire flickered gently in the grate, bathing the room in a shifting amber light.

"Rollo!" Asa hissed in his ear. "We should go back to bed."

He held his finger to his lips. "Listen," he whispered. He was thrilled by the idea that Skalti and Katla might get married. Uncle Skalti! He knew he would feel completely safe with an uncle like him around.

"That was a fine meal, Katla," Skalti was saying.

"Thank you."

Rollo turned to Asa with a told-you-so smile. She shook her head irritably. She still didn't believe him.

"I can't stay forever," Skalti said. "You've been too kind."

"Stay for as long as you like," Katla said. "Your shoulder—"

"It's healing well. I could leave tomorrow."

A long silence. Katla got up, and as she walked to the fireplace, the children could see her and shrank back behind the door.

"Don't go," Katla said.

"I've imposed on you too long."

"It's been my pleasure." Katla glanced down at her hands. "The children are very fond of you."

"Just the children?"

"No, not just the children."

Rollo saw Katla smile and Asa's eyes were as round as saucers. Now she believed him.

"Young Rollo is becoming a fine swordsman," Skalti said, and Rollo felt so proud that his chest swelled.

"Of course he is. As was his father," Katla answered. "A fine swordsman and a fine man."

"Are we going to tell them about Ragni?" Skalti continued, and the children looked at each other sharply.

"I don't think it's wise," Katla replied. "They'll want to find him. It's too dangerous. Especially after what happened last time."

Katla was referring to their recent adventure, when they'd only narrowly escaped from ghosts, tide stealers, and sea giants. But what did Skalti mean about Ragni, who had been his father's court sorcerer until the flood?

"I understand," Skalti said. "But those children are made of strong stuff. Asa is the heir to a great dynasty and Rollo is tough and smart. Ragni will know what happened to their parents—"

"Their parents are dead," Katla said forcefully.

"Are you sure?"

"Of course. Flood wouldn't have let them live."

"Ragni's alive. Flood let *him* live."

"Ragni's only barely alive," Katla said. "Trapped at Twistwater Point, only coming to his senses when the tide dips low. That's not living. I won't hear more of it, Skalti. I won't let the children risk their lives chasing the impossible."

Skalti fell silent, and soon they began to talk about other things. Glaring at Rollo, Asa quietly closed the door. "Don't get too excited."

"Did you hear him? He thinks Mama and Papa might still be alive."

"We'll talk about it tomorrow," she said.

"I want to talk about it now." He couldn't believe that she was being so cold. Didn't she long for her parents to return, just as much as he did? "Please, Asa, please."

"We must calm down and go to bed now," she said. But he could tell she wasn't calm. She fiddled with the Moonstone Star, the magic stone she'd inherited from their mother. Asa always wore it on a ribbon around her neck.

"But, Asa—"

"We'll need a good night's sleep," she said, "if we're going on an adventure tomorrow."

Rollo smiled. "You mean . . . ?"

"Of course. Tomorrow, we're going to find Ragni."

The next morning, they met in the field after breakfast. Asa felt nervous and jittery. She sat on a big, flat rock, but couldn't stop jiggling her feet. Rollo sat on the grass in front of her.

"So we're going to find Ragni?" he asked, and his voice was breathless with anticipation.

"Yes, we are, but you must listen to me very carefully," she said. With all the plans she had been making in her head, she had barely slept the night before. "First, you have to try not to get too excited. Mama and Papa are probably dead. We might not find Ragni and, even if we do find him, he might not be able to help us."

"I'll try," he said, but she could tell from the gleam in his eye that he was already far too excited.

"Second, we can't go today."

"What? Why?" Rollo asked.

Asa looked around, back up to the house where Katla hung washing on a rope between two lemon trees. "Aunt Katla is still angry with us because of last time. She's keeping an eye on us, Rollo. If we go anywhere near *Northseeker,* she'll see us and call us back. You heard what she said to Skalti. She doesn't want us to go."

"When are we going, then?"

"Tonight. When everybody's asleep."

Rollo nodded. "All right."

"So that means today we have to organize a few things. Two lanterns for the trip, extra blankets, and

furs. And we have to write a note to Aunt Katla, telling her where we've gone and asking her not to send anyone to find us."

"No one can find us, anyway," Rollo said. "*Northseeker* is invisible."

Asa checked over her shoulder again. Their aunt Katla had finished hanging out the washing and was approaching.

"I'll write the note," Asa whispered quickly. "You organize the supplies."

"What time will we leave?" Rollo asked.

"Midnight. Be ready."

The sky was clear, the quarter moon was pale, and the water was as black as midnight when they boarded *Northseeker* and pulled in the anchor. Rollo took the tiller while Asa pored over the maps by lamplight. The ship found its way out of the inlet, its cobweb sails motionless in the still night air.

"Here it is," Asa said at last, stabbing the map with

her finger. "Twistwater Point. It's southwest, around the flat islands."

"The outwaters," Rollo said, awed and a little frightened. Everyone knew that on the other side of the great islands lay vast empty spaces, with hardly any people or buildings in sight. It was a refuge for outlaws and supernatural creatures alike.

"Yes," Asa said, "the outwaters. We'll have to keep our wits about us. *Northseeker,* let's go."

With a gentle breath of magic, *Northseeker*'s sails fluttered and swelled. The ship skimmed forward, sailing them off into the night.

CHAPTER 2

THE OUTWATERS

Within two hours, *Northseeker* had left behind the gentle rolling hills of home, and was heading south to the outwaters. Clouds gathered, blotting out the dim starlight. Rain didn't fall; instead, a kind of grudging drizzle made the children miserable rather than wet. The air grew warmer and more humid, and the water continued unbroken as far as the eye could see.

Asa shrugged off her cloak. "It's sticky, isn't it?" she called to Rollo.

Rollo looked around. He was standing at the prow of the ship, straining his eyes into the dark. "I wish those clouds would blow away."

"We could always camp under the seats until it clears up."

"We'd lose too much time. We have to try to be home before Aunt Katla realizes we're gone."

"She'll realize we're gone soon. She always comes to check on us before dawn."

Rollo looked puzzled. "Does she? I didn't know that."

"Because you're always asleep."

He came back to sit with her as she held the tiller.

"Mama used to do it, too," Asa said softly.

"I don't remember."

"She always moved so lightly, but I woke up every time," she said, the memories making her feel sad and happy at the same time. "She'd go to your bed first and kiss you, then come to my bed, and I'd pretend I was asleep. She'd smooth the covers over my shoulders and leave again quietly."

Rollo was silent for a long time and Asa was afraid that she'd upset him. But when he turned his face up to her again, he was grinning broadly. "We might see her again, Asa."

"You shouldn't get your hopes up. . . ."

He rolled his eyes. "Just let yourself imagine it. What would you say to her?"

"I don't want to imagine it—not for a second. Because if it doesn't happen, I'll be sad all over again." She gazed off into the distance, looking for a distraction. "Can you see that?" she asked, pointing to a low-lying island on the horizon.

He leapt to the side of the boat. "That's the first land we've seen in ages."

"Is there anything on it?"

"No, it looks like mud. Maybe some rocks."

"Then it's the first of the flat islands. Behind them we'll find the outwaters. . . ."

"And in the outwaters we'll find Ragni."

"Yes," she said. "If we're not found by something else first."

On they sailed through the night. The clouds parted and the flat islands lay still under the weak moonlight. In the distance, Asa could occasionally hear the flapping wings of a great night bird, swinging off into the dark. She was very tired and her eyes were threatening to close. Rollo kept her awake with his excited chatter, and it was deep in the early hours of the morning when he went suddenly quiet and his eyes darted to the island they were passing.

"What's wrong?" she asked.

"Over there," he whispered.

Asa stood up so she could see more clearly. On the island, lying on a big rock, was some kind of lizard . . . or man . . . or . . .

"What is it?" she asked.

"I've read stories about creatures like that," Rollo said. "Horrible lizard men who do evil things."

Asa tried to make sense of the creature, which was sleeping and still. A lizard the size of a man, with

backward-jointed arms and legs, long fingers with pads on the end, smooth snake-like skin, and bulging eyes.

"You can't see his teeth," Rollo whispered. "But if what I've read is true, they are sharp."

"We must be very quiet," Asa said. "We're invisible to the real world, but the spirit world can see us on board *Northseeker.* I don't know whether those lizard men are spirits or not."

They sailed past and Asa held her breath the whole way. Without Rollo's chatter, the night was almost silent. Except for that faraway flapping of wings she had heard before. She turned and scanned the dark sky to see if she could spot the bird.

Rollo saw her puzzled face and followed her gaze. Up very high, a long way behind them, was a large gray bird, dipping and swooping. Following them.

Asa frowned and held her finger to her lips. As one flat island disappeared behind them, another loomed to starboard and she saw two more of the lizard men lying flat and motionless. As she looked closer, the dim moonlight made mocking shadows in the muddy landscape. There were more. She counted five; another only made itself visible when it stirred in its sleep. The lizard men were everywhere!

She drew Rollo close and pointed the creatures out to him. He clung to her, silent as the moon, as *Northseeker* sailed on.

That flapping again. Asa turned. Her long hair whipped across her eyes in a sudden breeze. The bird was closer now. Its wingspan was huge, its feathers ragged and gray. She noticed for the first time that its eyes glowed amber-red against the dark sky.

"I don't like the look of that thing," she whispered to Rollo.

He indicated with a shake of the head that he didn't, either. It drew closer, circling above *Northseeker.* Its glowing eyes were full of evil intent, and Asa was afraid it was planning to land on *Northseeker*'s mast.

"Here," she said softly to Rollo, and handed him the tiller.

As quietly as she could, she lifted the lid on the storage box beside it. All kinds of useful things had been stowed in here for their use, and her fingers closed around what she was after almost immediately.

A slingshot.

She took it and turned to Rollo. Her brother always had pockets full of pretty rocks that he had found. She held out her palm and he, seeing the slingshot, knew what to do. He gave her a flat black skimming stone.

She loaded it onto the slingshot. The bird drew closer. At this distance, Asa could see it had the body of an owl but the face of a cat. It wasn't just one set of glowing eyes that looked at her but two. When one set blinked, the other stayed open so that it never lost sight of the ship.

Asa pulled the slingshot and fired the rock into the sky. The bird guessed what she intended and turned on its wing, flapping up higher but not letting them out of its sight. Rollo handed Asa another rock and she shot again. The rock flew into the sky, knocking the bird on the wing. Its flight faltered and it landed on the muddy island.

All at once, there was noise and commotion. The

bird had landed in the center of a sleeping lizard-man community. The soft *whump* of its fall woke them and they descended on the creature with fury and hunger. Asa was appalled to see them tear the bird from each other, until its wings and head had been ripped off. They devoured it ravenously, their teeth staining with fresh blood.

She silently willed *Northseeker* to go faster. They were nearly past the tip of the island, and the lizard people hooted and howled as they fought over the bird. They were horrible to watch, running around on their odd backward-jointed legs, with their bulging eyes that blinked ever so slowly and their sharp teeth bared.

Asa released a deep breath as they slid out into open waters. The flat islands were behind them; the outwaters waited.

CHAPTER 3

SLEEPING THIEVES

A mist gathered around them: light at first, as fine as cobwebs, but then deepening into rolling clouds that clung to the water and swirled up around the ship.

"I can't see where we're going," Rollo complained, leaving his usual spot at the prow.

"We must be very close to Twistwater Point by now," Asa said. "*Northseeker,* slow. I don't want to run aground."

Persuaded by her caution, *Northseeker* slowed.

"I wonder if the sun will come up soon," Rollo said as he sat next to Asa.

"I think it's still a few hours away."

"I'm really sleepy."

"Me too."

"I wish that we'd . . ." He stopped talking, a puzzled expression coming over his face.

"What's the matter?" she said.

"Can you hear something?"

Asa strained her ears. Yes, she could. A rushing sound.

"What do you think it is?" she asked.

"It sounds like a waterfall . . . or a rainstorm . . ."

"Like water running fast . . ."

Suddenly *Northseeker* was buffeted by a big current. It surged up under them and tugged the ship off course; now the carved dragon on the prow was facing south-east instead of southwest.

"What happened?" cried Rollo.

"I don't know. I can't see."

The rushing sound grew louder and another current tore them violently back on course. Asa fell off her seat.

Rollo scampered back up to the prow and peered into the dark. The mist blanketed everything, but the rushing noise was directly ahead. It swirled and sucked and he didn't like the sound of it at all.

Then it dawned on him.

"Asa," he said quickly. "*Twist*water Point."

She followed his meaning and her face grew pale. "A whirlpool!" she gasped.

She took the tiller and wrenched it around. "Turn, *Northseeker,* turn!"

Northseeker turned. Another current from the whirlpool spiraled out and caught the prow, turning them back off course.

"No!" Asa cried, pulling the tiller as much as she could.

Rollo joined her, resting his hand over hers and pulling hard. "Come on, *Northseeker,* let's go," he said.

Northseeker strained against the currents that tugged the ship beneath them. Then its prow began to dip. The

mist parted suddenly and the children saw the whirlpool with frightening clarity. A deep funnel into the black water, half a mile across, its outer edge just a few yards ahead. And they were being dragged rapidly toward it.

Asa yelped and pulled even harder. *Northseeker* struggled against the current. The prow strained upward. Asa could see clearly that if they didn't turn immediately, the edge of the whirlpool was going to catch them and they would be heading down the steep slide in the water, whirling violently to their deaths. Her heart thundered. She had both hands on the tiller and so did Rollo, but it was jerking wildly and chaotically.

Asa took a deep breath. "We have to stay focused!" she shouted to Rollo over the rushing water.

His eyes were panicked. "Focused?"

"You, me, and *Northseeker.* Now listen." She tightened her grip. "On the count of three, we all pull together."

He nodded.

"One . . . two . . . three . . . *pull!*" she yelled.

They pulled; *Northseeker*'s magic pulled, too. The prow strained, then broke free of the current.

"Pull!" Asa screamed. "As hard as you can!"

The ship struggled, the edge of the whirlpool was barely a yard away, and now the stern of the ship was being drawn toward it.

"Go, *Northseeker.* Fast!" Asa yelled.

The cobweb sails fluttered; the edge of the whirlpool seemed to open up under them. *Northseeker* jerked forward and sprinted away so hard that Rollo fell over.

"We did it!" Asa cried joyfully.

Rollo picked himself up and ran to the stern of the boat, watching the whirlpool disappear behind them. "So if that's the Twistwater, where's the point?"

"It must be behind the whirlpool," Asa said, easing the tiller around. They entered the mist again. "We'll sail out a little farther, then go around in a wide arc."

"Let's keep as much distance between us and the whirlpool as we can."

"I intend to."

They found themselves skirting an island overgrown with trees and vines. As dawn glimmered on the horizon and the mist began to burn off, Rollo could see how strange these trees looked. Unlike the dark, broad-trunked, and round-leaved trees of home, these were tall and scrawny, with huge, flat leaves and odd swollen fruit growing on them. Long creepers trailed from the trees in untidy loops.

"Tell me when you see a good place to drop anchor," said Asa.

"It's too rocky here, but I think I can see a stretch of beach up ahead."

They sailed a few more minutes, then skidded up the sand and anchored *Northseeker.* Rollo built a small pyramid of rocks next to the ship so they could find it again on their return. It reminded him that while the ship would remain invisible, he and Asa would not.

"We have to be very careful," Asa said, thinking the same thing. "Stick together and stay close to the shadows." She tucked the Moonstone Star under her clothes and handed Rollo his cloak.

Rollo shrugged into it as he glanced toward the east, where the sun was a searing orange glow on the line of the horizon. "At least we'll be able to see where we're going," he said.

"And everything will be able to see us." She took his hand and they headed up the beach and into the tangled forest.

For a long time, there was nothing but the sound of their feet in the undergrowth, the morning breeze in the treetops, and the distant call of a bird. But after about an hour, Rollo thought he heard something else.

"Did you hear that?" he said to Asa.

She stopped to listen. "I don't hear anything."

"Like a shuffling noise." He listened hard but couldn't hear it anymore. "It's stopped."

"Maybe you imagined it."

They began to walk again, and as soon as they did, Rollo heard the noise once more.

"Shhh! I can hear it."

They stopped. The noise stopped. This was frustrating.

"Maybe it's an echo of our own footsteps," Asa said. "Or a—"

"HA!" With a sudden shout, a figure dropped from the tree in front of them.

A lizard man! It stank like saltwater and old cooking oil, and it bared its teeth and made ready to pounce.

"Run!" cried Asa, already turning on her heel. Rollo was right behind her, the lizard man snapping his jaws and reaching his sticky fingers toward them.

Rollo's heart beat fast. He swiped away overhanging vines that grazed his head and tried not to trip on roots and fallen branches. But the lizard man was much more nimble and gained on them quickly.

"Faster, Asa!" Rollo shouted.

"I'm going as fast as I can!"

Up ahead, a break in the trees revealed a sandy clearing. They burst through it, to find themselves running across the camp of five sleeping bodies. The commotion brought the bodies awake.

"Who's there?" called a voice.

"Help us!" cried Rollo.

Seconds later, all five of them were awake and had descended on the lizard man with gleaming swords. One was a raggedly dressed woman, with big, meaty arms and a dirt-streaked face. The other four were all men, half toothless, covered in faded tattoos, and dressed in layers of faded and torn clothes. The lizard creature fought against his captors, but was no match for five swords. Soon it lay dying in a pool of black blood.

"Thank you!" Asa gasped. "I don't know how we can—"

Her sentence was cut short when the ragged woman swiftly brought the tip of her sword around to press into Asa's chin. A drop of black blood dripped onto Asa's cloak. "Who are you and where are you going?" the woman asked. She stank of sweat and dirt.

Asa spoke in a clear voice. "We're just children, and we're lost. Can you guide us to Twistwater Point?"

The outlaw woman sneered. "Shall we believe them, boys?"

The others muttered in reply.

"Don't let 'em go, Skur."

"We could use a couple of new servants."

"See if they've got any gold."

Rollo felt his blood grow warm with rage. He was conscious of his sword, hidden under his cloak. Skalti had said he was a good swordsman, but even a good swordsman couldn't take on five armed outlaws and survive.

The woman, Skur, smiled unevenly at Asa and Rollo. "You know," she said to her men, "these children are wearing fine clothes. I bet they're worth something to somebody." She signaled with her hands, and an instant later, both children had been seized.

"Walk, children," Skur said, brandishing her sword. "If you do what we say, you won't get hurt."

CHAPTER 4

BAD MAGIC

The outlaws marched them for half an hour, and the whole time Rollo tried to figure out a way to get free. He glanced over to Asa, whose arms were twisted roughly behind her back. The outlaws who held her had their swords at the ready. Behind him, two more outlaws held their sword points against his back. If he walked too slowly, they pressed the blades firmly into his clothes to hurry him up. He thought really hard. If he turned on his own captors, then the outlaws who had Asa might hurt her. Skur was a few feet ahead, and she had sheathed her sword. Perhaps if he took her on . . . No, this was ridiculous. He was just a boy!

A break in the trees ahead signaled the end to their journey. Rollo had thought the other clearing was the outlaws' camp, but it was now obvious that it had only been a sleeping place while they were out hunting. Here were all their possessions—and so many of them! Trunks overflowing with clothes and jewels, plates and cups and richly decorated books. Many of the items were swollen and discolored with age and water. Katla had once told him about zammel birds, who collected all manner of pretty objects simply to decorate their nests. This is what the outlaws' camp reminded him of. They had all these objects but didn't appear to use them. He grew frightened: soon they would strip Asa and him of their clothes, and they would discover his sword. If he was going to act, it had to be soon.

But that fear was quickly overtaken by another.

Asa gasped and he followed her eyes to the far side

of the clearing, where a rough cage, about two yards across, hung from the trees. It was made of thin branches lashed together with vines, and inside it was a human skeleton.

"What do you intend to do with us?" Asa asked, her voice strained with fear.

The outlaws didn't answer. Rollo's heart thundered. These were bad people. They didn't care that Asa and Rollo were children. If he and his sister didn't escape now, they were going to die in that cage.

With shaking hands, he loosened the button on the front of his cape. He reached under it for his sword. Skur was leading her outlaw gang to the cage. Rollo leapt forward, pulling out his sword with a shout. The outlaws behind him tried to grab him, but only got a handful of his cloak as it slipped off his shoulders. He slashed out at Skur and cut one meaty arm. She howled and unsheathed her own sword. Out of the corner of his eye, Rollo saw that Asa's two captors had left her and turned on him.

"Run, Asa!" he shouted.

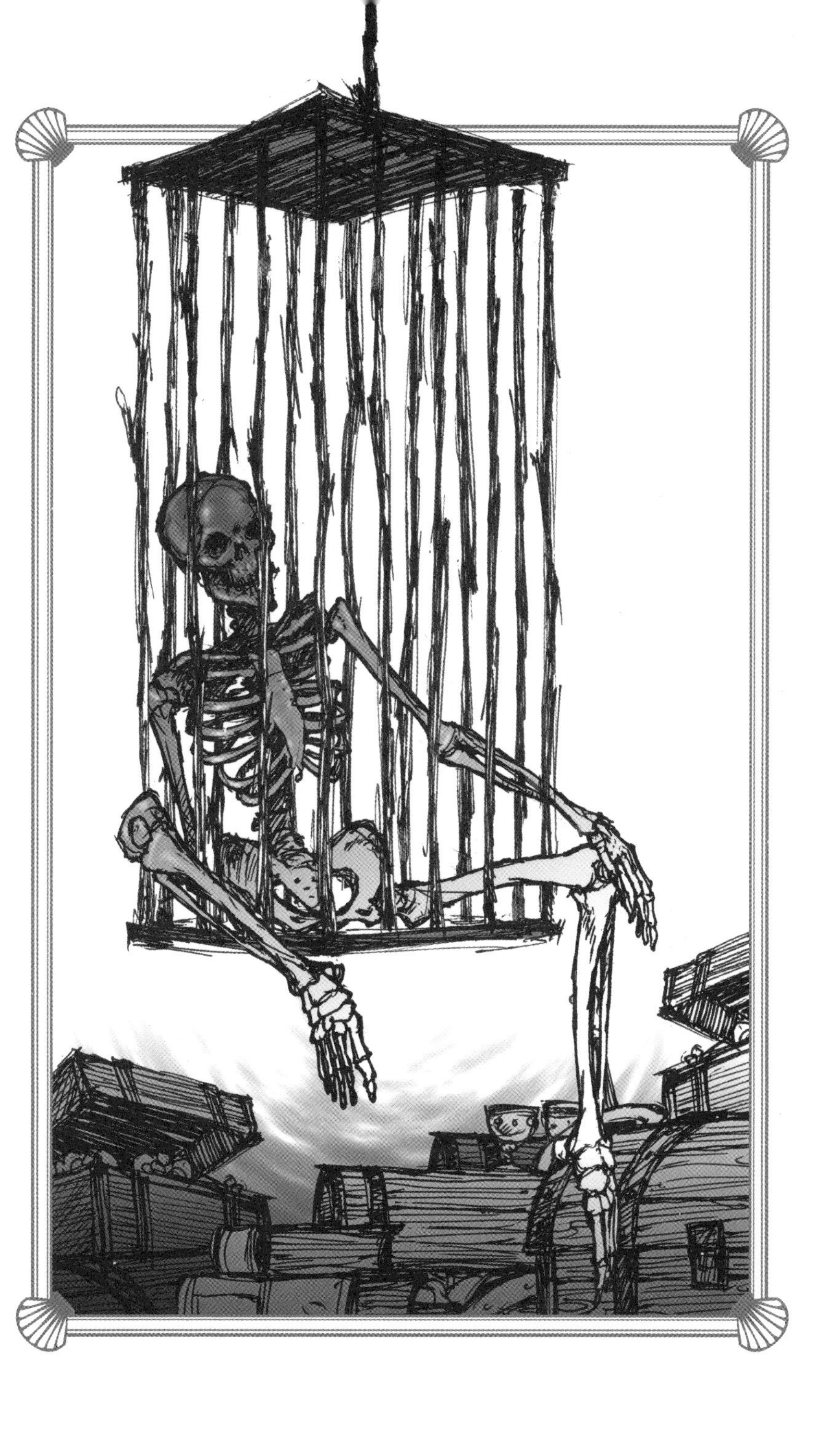

"Rollo! NO!" she screamed.

"Run. Go on!"

He couldn't tell whether she was convinced by the tone of his voice, or whether she had figured out that she could too easily be used as a hostage to make him drop his sword. Either way, she ran and disappeared into the trees.

Rollo had hurt Skur's sword arm, so she brandished her blade weakly. As soon as the other men had surrounded him, she dropped her sword, stood back to watch, and pressed her fingers tightly into her bleeding arm.

It all happened in such a blur that Rollo could never remember the details later. He took on the outlaw in front of him, who obviously thought he would be an easy foe. When Rollo blocked his blows and then knocked the outlaw's sword out of his hand, the other two closed in quickly. Now he was fighting both of them at once, but all his time was spent blocking their blows. He had no room for an attack of his own. Working in his favor was the fact that they had never fought anyone as short as him before and a number of deadly blows whizzed right above his head. But he was tiring, and the third outlaw had his sword and—

Suddenly a huge commotion burst from the trees: Asa was running hard and behind her were a dozen lizard men, trampling the undergrowth, bending and snapping branches as they tried to reach her. She stopped and held out her cloak, which was stained with black lizard blood, and they sniffed at it and howled. She threw it into the middle of Rollo's sword fight and the lizards descended.

"Come on, Rollo!" she shouted.

The lizards could smell Skur's blood now and it woke their appetites. Rollo's captors turned their attention to the lizard men and he was able to slip away. The lizard men were in such a frenzy over the cut on Skur's arm that they didn't notice, and the outlaws were too busy trying to free their leader. Asa grabbed Rollo's hand. Together they fled into the trees.

They ran and ran. Rollo nearly tripped over a low-hanging vine and Asa lost one of her shoes. But still

they ran, until the horrible sound of lizard men howling was well behind them. Then they slowed to a walk, panting and stunned.

"Will they come after us?" Rollo asked.

"Who? The lizard men or the outlaws?"

"Both. Either. This place is really dangerous, Asa."

"I know. Listen, can you hear the whirlpool?"

Rollo listened. He could. Faintly. The sound of rushing water.

"Let's follow the sound," she said. "We must be near the spot where Ragni is trapped by now."

They trudged on. "What did Aunt Katla say? That Ragni only comes to his senses when the tide is low? What do you think that means?"

"I don't know. Skalti once told me that Flood had allowed him to live, but at a terrible cost."

Rollo whipped around on her. "When did he say that?"

Asa wouldn't meet his eye. "That first day we met him, before he rescued you from the sea giants."

"So you've known all this time?"

"I didn't want to get your hopes up. I didn't know where Ragni was and—"

"Asa, that's not fair! You should have told me."

"I'm sorry."

"Is there anything else you haven't mentioned?"

She sighed. "No."

"Promise?"

"Yes. I'm sorry. I should have told you. But I don't think it will do any good to keep believing they're alive. Flood is evil; he wouldn't allow Mama and Papa to live."

"He let Ragni live."

"We don't know that for sure yet."

"*I* know it for sure. We're going to meet Ragni today. And if he let Ragni live . . ." Rollo said.

"Flood is torturing Ragni."

"But he's *alive*."

Asa waved the idea aside. "Look, no. One step at a time. If we find Ragni, we'll ask him, but I'm prepared for him to tell us that they're dead. Are you?"

Rollo considered this. He had to admit he wasn't: if

Ragni told him that Mama and Papa were dead, he was going to be horribly disappointed. He started to see Asa's point.

"All right," he said. "I'll try to be more sensible."

"Good."

Up ahead, the trees grew thinner and the sound of the whirlpool louder. As they moved clear of the forest, they could see a long, sandy strip of island like a white finger pointing out into the sea.

"That must be Twistwater Point," Asa said.

The sun was rising now and shone on the tip of a large black rock at the end of the point.

"I can't see Ragni," Rollo said, already disappointed.

"Maybe the tide isn't low enough." Asa sat on the sand, flicking her long dark hair off her face. "Let's sit here and watch."

"What if we've just missed the low tide? What if we have to wait until nighttime?"

Asa sat and removed her remaining shoe so she could put it in her pocket. "Then we'll wait."

Rollo wanted to say something about lizard men,

outlaws, and Katla's bad temper, but he remained quiet and sat with her as the day broke fresh and bright around them. The whirlpool kept spinning. Its constant rush was soothing and Rollo almost found himself nodding off to sleep.

After half an hour, Asa said firmly, "The tide is going out."

"How do you know?"

"Because when we first arrived, only the tip of the black rock was visible. Now I can see much more of it."

Rollo focused on the rock and watched closely. She was right: the tide was going out.

A sudden quietness surprised him. What was it?

"The whirlpool," she gasped.

And it was. The whirlpool was slowing down, the water growing smooth. The quiet that followed was heavy on his ears.

"What's happening?" he said.

"I don't know."

A strange black mist appeared to be rising from the now-still water, turning in circles as the whirlpool had done. The black rock shimmered and began to move. In the dark mist, Rollo thought he could see a ragged-winged bird like the one Asa had shot from the ship. Now there were two of them—four, eight! The mist resolved into horrible shapes: gray cat-faced birds, spindly armed spirits with howling mouths, squirming spike-fingered baby sea hags with screeching voices, and a dozen other unutterable creatures that were just misty shapes as black as the bad magic they were made from.

"Rollo," Asa said, "how come we can see them?"

"What do you mean?"

"I know that on *Northseeker* we can see spirits, but we shouldn't be able to see them now."

"Look!" he cried suddenly as his gaze was drawn back to the rock. The shimmering movement had stopped, and now they could see that tied to the black rock was a man, dressed in black robes, with a long black beard. At the exact moment he appeared, the black mist sucked in on itself and dissolved, taking all the magical horrors with it.

"Ragni!" Rollo gasped. "It has to be."

Asa pulled herself to her feet. "Let's go."

CHAPTER 5

ACROSS THE POINT

Now that the whirlpool was quiet, the only sounds were of the waves gently rushing onto the shore and the songs of birds waking for the day. The sand was soft under Asa's bare toes. She kept her eyes focused on the black rock at the end of the sandy point and tried not to think about what would happen next. What would Ragni tell them? Would he know anything? What if he knew nothing? What if he confirmed that Mama and

Papa were dead? Despite her warnings to Rollo, she, too, had begun to hope that her parents might still be alive. She feared the moment of disappointment almost as much as she feared the outlaws with their sharp blades and creaking cage.

A sudden sharp barb to the bottom of her foot surprised her.

"Ouch!" she cried, and sat down. A burning sensation had started in her foot and was growing hotter and more painful with each passing second.

"What is it?" Rollo asked.

"Something bit me." She scanned the white sand, but at first couldn't see anything. Then a tiny movement caught her eye. "There!" She pointed.

Rollo gasped. "Oh no!"

"What is it?"

"A sea spider."

Trying to distract herself from the pain, Asa focused on the movement. A ghostly white spider, half the size of her hand, with spindly legs and a milky body, scurried away down a hole in the sand.

"I've never heard of sea spiders," she said quietly, squirming against the burning pain in her foot.

Rollo sat next to her and examined the bite with concern. "They only live in warmer climates. Asa, they're really poisonous. When they bite, they leave a spine in the wound that keeps pumping poison in after they're gone. We have to get it out."

"Don't touch it! It's agony."

"I have to touch it. I have to get the spine out. Hold still."

Asa braced herself while Rollo got a grip on the tiny spine. The lightest touch sent bolts of pain shooting up her leg. Finally, as he pulled it out, the pain began to ease.

"There!" he said, holding up the spine for her to look at.

"Throw it in the water," she said. "I don't want to stand on it again."

He went to the edge of the point and threw the poisonous spine into the water. Asa's eyes were drawn upward to a dark shape coming closer and closer.

"Rollo!" she cried, scrambling to her feet.

But he had seen it, too. A sky patrol! One of Flood's dark balloons full of spies.

Sure enough, the horribly familiar hiss of the balloon filling with hot air came to their ears. It had been masked by the sound of the waves.

Sssshhhhhhhhhhhhhhhhhh.

"I think they've already seen us," Rollo said, frozen to the spot.

"They're too far away."

"They have their telescopes out, pointed at us."

"What do we do? Run back to the island? What if the outlaws get us?"

"Or the lizard men."

"There's only one thing we can do," she said grimly.

He nodded. "Breath of a fish within me!" he declared, and jumped into the water.

Asa took a deep breath and spread her arms. "Wings of a raven upon me!"

At once the miraculous transformation began. Her body buzzed with strange energy, her bones grew small and light, feathers sprouted black and glossy. A moment later, she took to the sky, swooping up in an arc above Ragni. The old sorcerer was watching her with keen eyes: it was his magic, after all, that made the children's enchantments possible.

But something terrible was happening. The sky patrol must have seen her transform to a raven, because now they were following her!

Asa flapped her wings madly, the big balloon hard on her tail. She swooped back down to the island, ducking between trees and vines to find a shady grove to hide. The sky patrol hovered overhead. She could hear their voices calling to each other.

"Did you see which way she went?"

"Land this thing. We'll find her easier that way."

"I'm not landing on that island. It's infested with bad magic."

"We'll send a rope down, then."

Sssshhhhhhhhhhhhhhhhhh. The balloon filled.

She listened in horror as they made a plan to send a spy down, attached to a rope so they could pull him up

quickly if necessary. Surely she'd be able to outrun them? But if she stayed too long as a bird, she would be terribly sick upon returning to her own body.

Worse—what if they captured her?

She waited tensely, perched on a branch in the grove. She sat as close to the trunk of the tree as she could, but wished for the big, spreading trees of home. These thin trees with their huge leaves let too much light in; she was afraid she would be seen. Long minutes passed as they organized themselves and decided who would go down the rope. Maybe she should fly back to *Northseeker*? No—if they saw her, they would know about the invisible ship, too. What about Rollo? He had gone underwater right where the whirlpool of bad magic waited.

Just then a flock of blackbirds flew in arrow formation overhead. There was a sudden commotion as ropes were pulled back in and the balloon took off. Asa watched in horror as they rose into the sky and gained on the birds. One of the spies sent out a huge net and the birds all tumbled into it. That was the last she saw before the balloon turned and headed back the way it had come, its awful hiss retreating into the distance.

Asa felt like she could breathe again. She could almost laugh as she thought of the spies taking a net full of birds to Flood, only to discover they were ordinary blackbirds. But she would have to be much more careful when using her enchantment in the future.

She took to the sky and headed back to the point, back to Ragni's rock.

CHAPTER 6

THE GUARDIAN WYRM

Meanwhile, under the water, Rollo began to swim carefully for the end of the point, keeping his eye out for spirits and other bad magic. The water was clear, the floor sandy and white. The sun illuminated the whole scene. There were no fish living here, no seaweed grew, not even shells decorated the bottom of the sea. Probably nothing could live so close to the whirlpool.

As he swam farther up the point, he noticed that the

sandy sea floor dropped away sharply into a trench. He paused on the edge, cautiously peering across the chasm. It was carved in a huge circle: the same shape as the whirlpool itself. Its murky depths were not visible. Rollo looked up. He could see Ragni's feet above him and for the first time saw that Ragni was tied to the black rock.

Just ropes? Surely he and Asa would be able to get him free.

Rollo swam upward, curious, reaching for the ropes around Ragni's leg. Ragni's foot twitched as though he wanted to kick out. Rollo didn't understand what the sorcerer was trying to signal, but he didn't want to surface until the sky patrol was definitely gone. He touched the rope again, and immediately a deafening, high-pitched squeal echoed down into the water. He would have put his hands over his ears, but he needed them to keep swimming so he wouldn't fall to the bottom of the trench. He shook his head, trying to shake the awful noise off. He was so distracted that he didn't notice the shadow behind him until it was too late.

He turned. Rearing up out of the murky trench was a sea monster! It looked like a giant pink worm, with slimy skin that pulsed as its muscles moved. In the center of its head was a single black eye, easily as big as Rollo himself, and right now that eye was focused on him. Beneath the eye, a mouth snapped open, filled with rows and rows of needle-like teeth. Rollo remembered from his books that this was called a wyrm, and that they were most often used to guard treasure.

Rollo tried to swim backward, but the wyrm was long and continued to uncoil, leisurely and unhurried, toward him. Rollo feared it could follow him all the way back to the beach without any trouble at all.

Ragni was waving his feet frantically, but Rollo had no idea what the old magician was doing. He was too far from the rock now to surface and ask, so he had to figure this out by himself. But the wyrm drew closer, the awful high-pitched squeal confused him, and the sky patrol waited above.

Rollo drew his sword.

Now that he was out of the trench, he could stand

on the seafloor, so he rested his feet and faced the wyrm head-on. The big eye hovered in front of him, blinking slowly. Rollo was transfixed, telling himself to be brave as it drew closer.

Without warning, something grabbed him. He cried out. He hadn't seen the long, fine tendril that shot out of the wyrm's side. Now it wrapped around him like a sickly pink vine and dragged him back to the trench.

"No, you don't!" he shouted, but his words turned soft and bubbly underwater. He slashed at the tendril and it snapped and fell off, issuing cloudy purple blood. In an instant, another tendril was around him, and another. They uncurled from the sides of the wyrm and held him fast around the waist and legs. Rollo lashed out madly, but for every tendril that he cut, another appeared.

Now the wyrm had him at the edge of the trench. Rollo couldn't see how deep it was through the dark water. The beast itself was coiled around and around into the murky shadows, and Rollo got the impression that the trench might even be bottomless. Slowly but surely, the wyrm was dragging Rollo down into that endless darkness. Would he be crushed? Or eaten?

The wyrm watched him with that big blinking eye the whole time and began to draw him closer. When its mouth opened, the needle teeth were clearly visible.

Rollo changed his strategy. Rather than slashing at the tendrils, he pulled his sword close to his body, point upright, and waited. The wyrm now began to draw him toward its mouth. He could feel his heart thundering under his ribs. Too easily, he could imagine how sharp those teeth were. He didn't want to die. He wanted to see Asa again and his baby sister, Una, and he wanted to find his parents.

"I won't die," he said firmly, and he gripped his sword.

The wyrm's mouth stretched wide, as though it intended to eat Rollo in one bite. He was close enough to feel the pulse of the warm water expelled through its gills.

Then he struck. One swift blow, directly into the wyrm's eye. The hard outer layer of the eye gave way to squishy jelly; the sword went in and purple blood began to pour out.

All its tendrils withdrawing immediately, the wyrm howled. Rollo was free. He swam up as fast as he could as it flicked its head this way and that, trying to shake the sword free, too. But it stuck and, swaying in jerky movements, the wyrm began to falter.

Finally, it sagged forward, its great head coming to rest on the sandy seafloor. Then the weight of its body caused it to collapse, dead, back into the trench.

Relief flooded through Rollo, relaxing all his muscles. He looked up. Ragni's feet were still. He wondered whether the sky patrol was gone. He decided to swim to the surface and take a quick peek.

Letting just the top of his head break the surface, he checked the sky. No patrol. Asa, still in her raven shape, was flapping toward him. He looked over at Ragni and noticed that the tide had risen: the water was now up to his thighs.

Then the magician spoke. "Hurry, children," he said. "We don't have much time."

Rollo climbed out of the water and sat on the sand next to Ragni's rock. Asa transformed herself and sat next to him. The nausea started immediately. Every time they used their enchantments, they got sick afterward. And it seemed to be getting worse.

"I suppose you have many questions," Ragni said. He was a big man, with a black beard and dark, hooded eyes.

Asa clutched her stomach and said to Ragni, "The first thing I want to know is why you let these enchantments make us so sick."

Ragni frowned. "It's because you're children. The same enchantments on adults would have no effect. It's like medicine. A dose that's right for an adult would be too much for a child."

"Then why didn't you give us a smaller dose?" Rollo asked.

"Because I didn't know how long you would need the enchantments. You might still need them as adults."

Ragni's eyes grew even darker as a grim expression shadowed his face. "Does your aunt Katla teach you healing, Asa?"

She nodded.

"So you will know that too much medicine can make a patient sick. What happens if too much medicine is given to a patient repeatedly?"

Asa thought about this, then said firmly, "They die."

"That's right."

Rollo was horrified. "So these enchantments could kill us?"

"Eventually. You will get sicker and sicker each time you use them, and one day . . . So be wise, children. Use your enchantments only as a last resort."

Rollo suddenly had to throw up. He ran back up the beach and vomited in the sand. It made him feel a little better. When he returned, Asa was lying on her side. He snuggled up in front of her, with her arm over his shoulder.

"You have other questions, I take it?" Ragni said, this time with a smile that transformed his face. Now he seemed gentle and kind. "Very important questions."

Rollo was so afraid he could barely voice it, but it was the question he'd come all this way to ask. "Ragni," he stammered, "are Mama and Papa . . . I mean, are they . . . still alive?"

Ragni looked puzzled. "Of course. Of course they are."

CHAPTER 7

RAVENS IN CAGES

Asa was shocked into silence. It didn't seem real. Mama and Papa still alive?

"Where?" she spluttered at last. "Where are they?"

"They're in the dungeons deep in the bowels of Castle Crag. In separate cells so they can't speak to one another. Still very much alive."

Asa looked at Ragni dubiously. "How do you know that?" she said. "You've been trapped here for a year.

How do you know that they're still alive?"

"Because the floods are still upon the land," he said. "Do you not understand? Flood used your mother's magic to raise the waters: his was not strong enough. If she were dead, the water would recede."

"And Papa?"

"Flood keeps your father alive because he stops your mother from ending her own life and reversing the flood. Your mother is a noble and brave woman, Asa. She couldn't endure the suffering of her people for long. Her love for your father, and for you, is the only thing keeping her alive."

Asa fell silent as she took all this in.

"How did Flood get Mama's magic?" Rollo asked.

"He stole it. The whole time he was in your parents' service, he was working on a new science, to extract magic, just as a weasel sucks the yolk from an egg."

Asa noticed that the tide was rising fast. She was completely overwhelmed by feelings and fears. She hadn't slept in two days and everything seemed like a dream. On the one hand, there was the joy that her parents were alive. On the other, there was the fear that her enchantments could kill her; that somehow she and Rollo had to get back to the other side of the island to find *Northseeker.* Then, when they got home . . . She closed her eyes and sighed.

"I know that the responsibility is heavy, Asa," Ragni said to her. "But you *will* have to go and find your mother and father. Nobody else can do it. Flood has them hidden under an enchantment. The guards who attend them simply see ragged thieves. Only their children, those who love them most, will be able to see their true faces." Ragni shifted uncomfortably in his bonds. "I wish I could help you."

"Is there any way you can get free?" asked Rollo.

"If anybody touches the ropes, the guardian wyrm comes."

"But I just killed it," boasted Rollo.

Ragni shook his head. His beard was trailing in the water now. "When the tide rises again and the bad magic starts the whirlpool, it will be stirred from its grave and reborn. Trust me, it's *very* bad magic in this place. So intense that even the natural eye can see it."

"What about your magic?" Asa asked. "Do you have any left at all?"

"None. Flood extracted it all."

Asa thought about the Moonstone Star under her shirt. She couldn't use it—she was too young—but perhaps Ragni could.

No, it was too special to give away.

"What happens to you when the tide comes in?" Rollo asked.

"I become part of this rock. I can't move, but I can think. I fear it will eventually drive me mad." The water lapped at his bottom lip. "Children, there isn't much time. First, let me call *Northseeker.*" He pressed his lips together and made a slow whistling sound. "You'll have to sail before the tide goes over my head. Then the bad magic will start again and the whirlpool will suck you into the trench. Be careful." He stretched his neck to keep his mouth clear of the water.

"Is there anything else we need to know?" Asa asked desperately.

"No, I can't give you more detail than this. I never saw your parents' prison, but the dungeons are below the castle." He smiled tenderly. "I can tell you this: if you always go forward with love in your hearts, you will make your parents' proud."

Finally, the water was too high and Ragni gasped a quick "Go!"

"Where's *Northseeker*?" Rollo asked.

He indicated the sand next to them with his eyes. Rollo leapt to his feet and began to feel the air in front of him. "Found it!" he cried, and climbed into the boat.

Asa was about to do the same when she turned and looked back at Ragni. His black eyes were still above the water, watching her.

Her fingers went to her neck and pulled off the Moonstone Star. She moved to Ragni.

"Here," she said, slipping the ribbon over his head. "You may be able to use this."

Ragni nodded, his eyes filling with grateful tears. Then the water slipped up again and he had to close them.

Asa ran for *Northseeker* and climbed on board. Rollo was already pulling in ropes and adjusting the tiller. On the water, a faint hint of black mist started swirling.

"We'd better be quick," Asa said.

"I know."

They pulled away from the point as water started slowly swirling again. When Asa took a last look behind her, Ragni had disappeared once more into his rock prison. The mist lay thick, the bad magic danced in circles, the whirlpool rushed to life. *Northseeker* moved fast, its cobweb sails fluttering.

Asa lay down in the bottom of the boat, sick and exhausted. Rollo smiled at her. "Which way is home?"

"You know," she said.

"Yes. I just want you to say it."

"North," she said, puzzled.

"And which direction does *Northseeker* travel without our help?"

"North," she answered with a smile.

He lay down next to her and within minutes they were both asleep.

As they sailed back into the inlet near Two Hills Keep, Asa saw a lone figure pacing in the grass.

"It's Aunt Katla," she said to Rollo.

Rollo came to stand next to her. "We're in so much trouble."

They pulled in to shore and threw down the anchor. Rollo was still tying ropes as Asa jumped off *Northseeker* and called, "Aunty Katla!"

Katla turned, worry and anger in her eyes. "Asa, where's your brother?"

"He's here, too." Just then Rollo appeared. He crouched to set a pile of stones next to *Northseeker*'s gangplank.

Katla hurried toward them. "What on earth were you thinking? I've been worried sick! You could have been killed! Don't you ever—"

"Aunty Katla," Rollo interrupted, unable to keep the smile off his face. "Aunty Katla, they're alive."

Katla stopped, her eyes round with surprise.

"It's true," Asa said. "They're imprisoned at Castle Crag. We have to go and—"

"You're not going anywhere," Katla said. "Never again. I'll lock you in your room if I have to."

"We've got to go!" protested Rollo. "Only Asa and I can save them."

"If we save them, we save the whole kingdom from Flood."

Katla sighed and shook her head. "This is all too much for me. We'll ask Skalti for advice when he gets back. He's gone to find a ship." Katla gave them a stern glance. "A ship to find you with. I suppose he won't need it now."

Rollo grinned. "Do you think he would come with us? When we go to rescue Mama and Papa?"

Katla took his arm and Asa's, too. She held them both tightly and was silent for a moment. Then she said, "There are dangers that you children aren't aware of."

"But we've faced dangers and we're fine and we're—"

"No, listen. Everywhere in the Star Lands, people

are trapping ravens in cages. At market today I saw six. Flood is paying a gold piece for every trapped raven. The rumor is that he is drowning them in their cages. Hundreds of dead ravens have washed up on the islands near Castle Crag."

Asa's blood chilled. "He knows?" she said. Of course, the sky patrol would have told him.

"Oh yes," Katla said. "Flood knows. He knows you children are meddling in his affairs. He knows you have enchantments." Her skin was pale and her eyes serious. "Children, Flood is determined to find you."

THE
SUNKEN
KINGDOM
4
THE
STAR QUEEN
Kim Wilkins
Illustrated by
D. M. Cornish

Asa and Rollo's adventures continue in . . .

THE SUNKEN KINGDOM BOOK FOUR

THE STAR QUEEN

Asa awoke when the world shook.

She had been sleeping in the soft, peaceful dark. Then came the crack of an explosion, a white-hot flash, and the shuddering of the ground beneath Two Hills Keep. Her eyes flew open and she sat up.

"What was that!" she gasped.

Rollo was climbing out of the bed next to her. Little Una, their baby sister, started to cry.

Asa dashed to the window and threw back the shutters. In the distance, beyond the hills, a fiery light flickered.

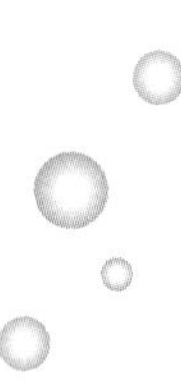

ABOUT THE AUTHOR

Since the publication of her first novel, *The Infernal,* in 1997, Kim Wilkins has established herself as a leading fantasy author in Australia and internationally. Her books include *Grimoire*, *The Resurrectionists*, *Angel of Ruin*, *The Autumn Castle,* and *Giants of the Frost.* She has also written a series for young adults about a psychic detective. She lives in Brisbane, Australia.

Kim's first novel, *The Infernal,* won both the horror and fantasy novel categories of the Aurealis Awards in 1997.

ABOUT THE ILLUSTRATOR

After graduating from the University of South Australia, David Cornish took his portfolio to Sydney, where he found work with several magazines and newspapers. Three years later, an opportunity arose there to be on the drawing team of the game show *Burgo's Catchphrase*. After six years with the show, David became restless, circumnavigating the globe before returning to Adelaide, Australia.

David's bold, graphic style and fine draftsmanship have made him a successful illustrator in Australia, and in the United States he is best known as both the author and the illustrator of the fantasy series Monster Blood Tattoo.

THE SUNKEN KINGDOM